D0903167

DISCARD

JP Pym   R & R

Pym, T.
Have you ever seen a sneep?.

PRICE: $24.95 (3559/go   )

For Olivia and her lovely mum, Lisa
T.P.

For Crista
J.S.

HAVE YOU EVER SEEN A SNEEP?
A DOUBLEDAY BOOK 978 0 385 61283 8

Published in Great Britain by Doubleday,
an imprint of Random House Children's Books
A Random House Group Company

This edition published 2009

1 3 5 7 9 10 8 6 4 2

Text copyright © Tasha Pym, 2009

Illustrations copyright © Joel Stewart, 2009

The right of Tasha Pym and Joel Stewart to be identified as the
author and illustrator of this work has been asserted in accordance with
the Copyright, Designs and Patents Act 1988.

All rights reserved.

RANDOM HOUSE CHILDREN'S BOOKS
61–63 Uxbridge Road, London W5 5SA

www.**kids**at**randomhouse**.co.uk
www.**rbooks**.co.uk

Addresses for companies within The Random House Group Limited can be found at:
www.randomhouse.co.uk/offices.htm
THE RANDOM HOUSE GROUP Limited Reg. No. 954009

A CIP catalogue record for this book is available
from the British Library.

Printed and bound in Singapore

Have You Ever Seen a SNEEP?

Tasha Pym

Illustrated by
Joel Stewart

DOUBLEDAY

Have you ever set out
a picnic in a truly
splendid spot,

turned your back
for just one second . . .

. . . to find a Sneep
has pinched the lot?

Have you ever wanted some quiet,
a little time to read a book,

settled down beneath a tree . . .

. . . to have it
ruined by a Snook?

hen I bet you've been
down by a stream,
playing on a rope,

swung out
and over the water . . .

. . . and straight down
a Grullock's throat?

Surely you've spied a Knoo and thought,
"Of all the curious things!"

Gone in to take a closer look . . .

. . . to discover
that it springs?

You simply *must* have been out walking then,
maybe whistling a tune,

just going about your business . . .

. . . then been chased
home by a Loon?

Now, wait . . .
please let me get this straight.

Where you live there are no Grullocks

or Sneeps?

No Snooks?

No Loons?

No Knoo?

Well then, I hope that you
won't mind, because . . .

. . . I'm coming
to live with you!